COWPOKE CLYDE RIDES THE RANGE

LORI MORTENSEN ILLUSTRATED BY MICHAEL ALLEN AUSTIN

Clarion Books | Houghton Mifflin Harcourt | Boston   New York

To Martin, who always nails his rides
and has met his share of critters along the way
—L.M.

For Cile and Jack
—M.A.A.

Clarion Books

215 Park Avenue South

New York, New York 10003

Text copyright © 2016 by Lori Mortensen

Illustrations copyright © 2016 by Michael Allen Austin

Clarion Books is an imprint of

Houghton Mifflin Harcourt Publishing Company.

The text was set in Grandma.

The illustrations were executed in acrylic, colored pencil,

and digital on Strathmore 500 series illustration board.

Book design by Sharismar Rodriguez

www.hmhco.com

Library of Congress Cataloging-in-Publication Data is available.

ISBN 978-0-544-37030-2

Manufactured in Malaysia

TWP 10 9 8 7 6 5 4 3 2 1

4500575418

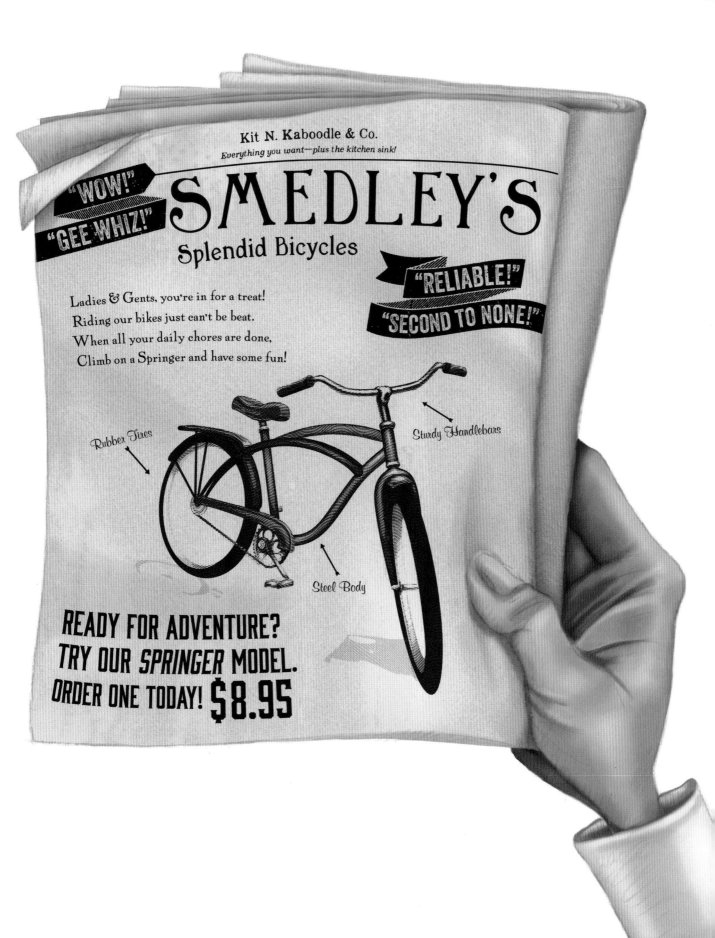

COWPOKE CLYDE poked at an ad.
"Looky, Dawg, at this here fad.
It says that when my chores are done,
I'm s'posed to ride a bike fer fun."

Ride a bike? It weren't no horse!
He'd have to try it out, of course.
"Imagine *me* a-ridin' 'round
on two big wheels across the ground."

The more Clyde thunk, the more he smiled
at ridin' something not so wild.
It wouldn't eat. It wouldn't stray.
It wouldn't buck or bite or neigh!

So with a wink at his ol' Dawg . . .

Clyde bought one from the cat-y-log.

When it came, the one he'd seen,
he strode around his steel machine.
"Piece of cake," said Cowpoke Clyde.
"I think I'll take it fer a ride."

Clyde plopped down on the skinny seat
and pushed the pedals with his feet.

As he rolled, he picked up speed
on his strange newfangled steed,
wibblin', wobblin' down the road,
right straight at a . . .

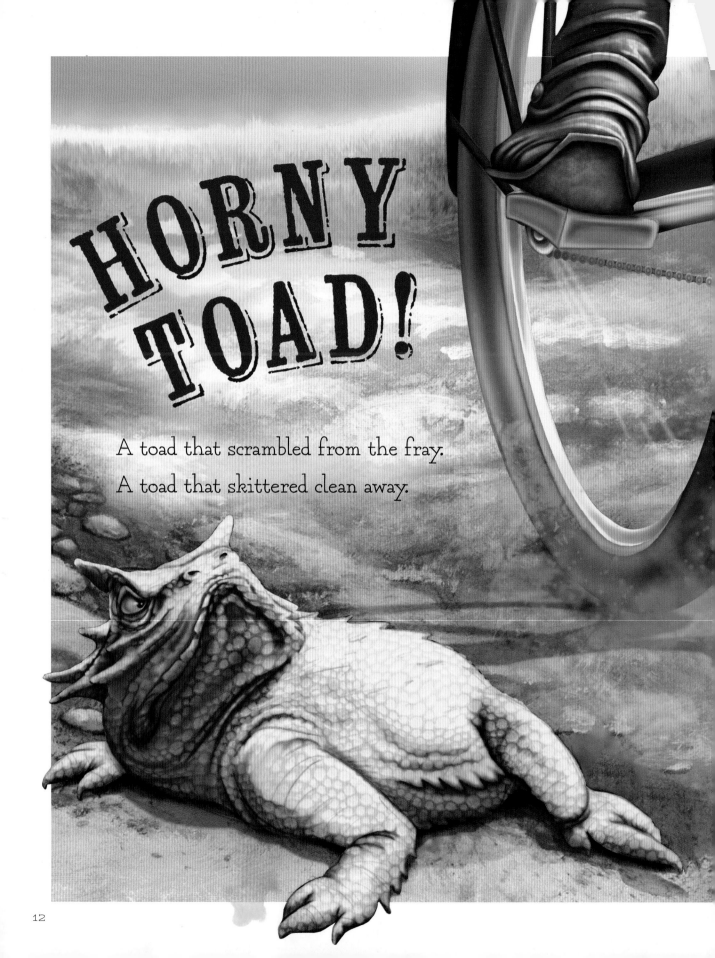

HORNY TOAD!

A toad that scrambled from the fray.
A toad that skittered clean away.

Ziggin', zaggin' left and right,
Clyde bump-bump-BUMPED and held on tight,
wishing for some trusty reins
to steer this thing across the plains.

Then all at once, caught unaware,
Clyde blundered toward a long-eared . . .

HARE!

A hare that stared with bugged-out eyes.
A hare that leaped in sheer surprise.

"Look out!" cried Clyde. "I'm comin' through!"
If only he knew what to do.
Brakin'? Steerin'? How'd it work?
Ridin' bikes was plumb berserk!

As beads of sweat rolled down his spine,
he hurtled toward a . . .

PORCUPINE!

A porcupine with spiky quills.
A porcupine that gave Clyde chills.

Would the beast and Clyde collide?
"I'm done fer now!" the cowpoke cried.

Swervin' left, then swervin' right,
he jerked the bars with all his might,
launched his bike into the air,
and cleared the quills with scant to spare.

He landed—*SMACK!*—right in the dirt,
rubbed his seat, wiped off his shirt,
and gave the bike a nasty kick.
He didn't like it. Not one lick!

"Who cares about a tomfool ride
on some ol' bike?" cried Cowpoke Clyde.

He grabbed his hat and started back,
heading for his comfy shack.
But as he walked, he thunk a bit.
How could a cowpoke up and quit?

So like it was an ornery horse,
Clyde went back to his bike, of course.
Legs or wheels, hooves or spokes,
he'd nail this ride—like all cowpokes!

Clyde mounted up, set out again,
dashin' down a hill—and then,
with one foolhardy, frenzied leap,
he shot straight for some bighorn . . .

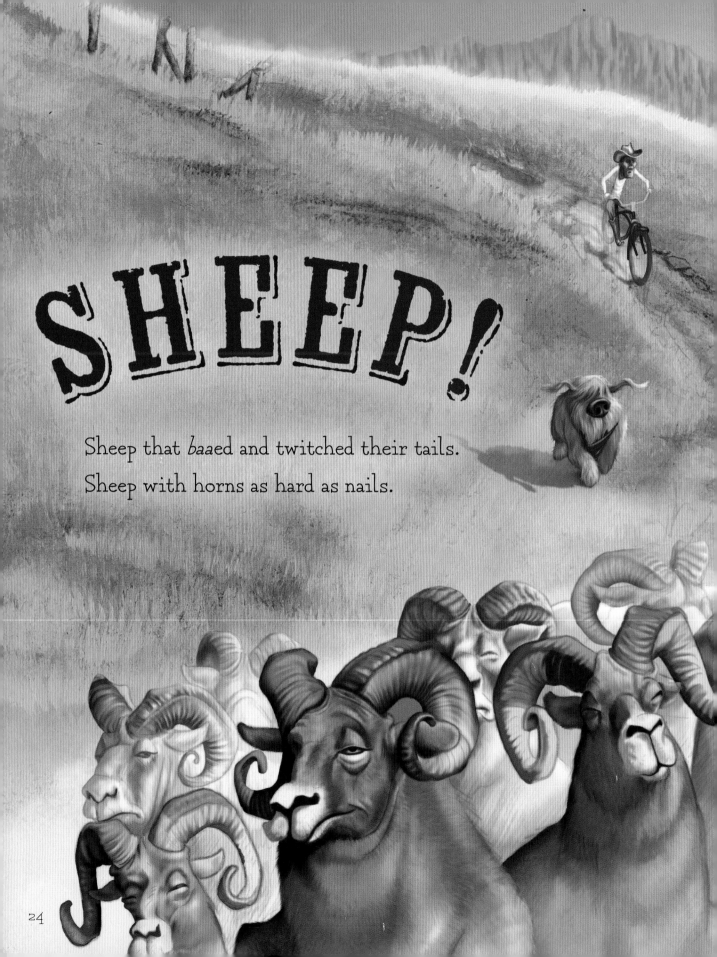

SHEEP!

Sheep that *baaed* and twitched their tails.

Sheep with horns as hard as nails.

But like a train upon a track,
Clyde had no way to turn on back.
Bouncin', boundin' down the hill,
he was doomed fer sure, until . . .

Ol' Dawg, his howlin', growlin' hound,
raced across the windswept ground,
scatterin' sheep as Clyde shot through.
Clyde skidded to a stop—

YAHOO!

He didn't crash. He didn't fall.
In fact, he weren't half bad at all.

Soon, he was ridin' like a pro
in some two-wheeled rodeo.
"It ain't *that* hard," said Cowpoke Clyde,
"when you take it all in stride."

Now whenever chores are done,
Clyde rides his steel machine fer fun.
Who rides with him across the ground?
Of course—his faithful, furry . . .